To Finn,

it was all your idea!

—B. W.

Published by

Peachtree Publishers

1700 Chattahoochee Avenue

Atlanta, Georgia 30318-2112

www.peachtree-online.com

Text and illustrations © 2018 by Bethan Woollvin

First published in Great Britain in 2018 by Two Hoots, an imprint of Pan Macmillan

First United States version published in 2018 by Peachtree Publishers

The illustrations were rendered in gouache on cartridge paper.

Printed in April 2018 in China

10 9 8 7 6 5 4 3 2 1

First Edition

HC ISBN: 978-1-68263-073-0

Library of Congress Cataloging-in-Publication Data

Names: Woollvin, Bethan, author, illustrator.

Title: Hansel & Gretel / Bethan Woollvin.

Other titles: Hansel and Gretel

Description: First edition. | Atlanta, Georgia : Peachtree Publishers, 2018. | "First published in Great Britain in 2018 by Two Hoots, an imprint of Pan Macmillan"—Title page verso. | Summary: In a fairy tale twist, Hansel and Gretel ransack Willow the good witch's gingerbread cottage and play havoc with her spells, driving the poor witch to her wit's end.

Identifiers: LCCN 2017057254 | ISBN 9781682630730

Subjects: | CYAC: Witches—Fiction. | Brothers and sisters—Fiction.

Classification: LCC PZ7.1.W67 Han 2018 | DDC [E]—dc23 LC record available at *https://lccn.loc.gov/2017057254*

Bethan Woollvin

Hansel & Gretel

PEACHTREE
ATLANTA

Deep in the forest, in a home made entirely out of gingerbread, there lived a witch named Willow. Willow wasn't like most witches.

She only used good magic, because Willow was a good witch.

One day, while she was out in the forest, Willow spotted a trail of bread crumbs. She decided to follow it.

At the end of the trail, she found
two children.

"We're Hansel and Gretel," one said.

"What do you want?" the other demanded.

"I'm worried these bread crumbs might lead birds and mice to my gingerbread home," said Willow. "Please, could you help me clean them up?"

Hansel and Gretel didn't like this idea, so they left Willow to tidy up on her own. But Willow did not get angry, because Willow was a good witch.

When she arrived home, Willow couldn't believe her eyes.

"Hansel, Gretel, please don't eat my house!" she cried.

"It's so tasty!" Gretel said through a mouthful of gingerbread.

But Willow did not get angry, because Willow was a good witch.
Hansel and Gretel must be very hungry, she thought. So she
invited them in for dinner.

While Hansel and Gretel made themselves at home, Willow used her best and most delicious spells to cook up a feast for them all.

"Please save some for me," said Willow.

When Willow got to the table, however, she found that Hansel and Gretel had already gobbled up all of the food!

But Willow did not get angry, because Willow was a good witch.

It wasn't long before Willow had more to worry about than her rumbling tummy.

Hansel and Gretel found Willow's spells and wands and began to play with them.

"Hansel, Gretel, please be careful with my magic things!" she cried.

Hansel and Gretel did not listen to Willow.

The magic grew and grew. . .

. . . and grew!

Hansel and Gretel wanted the house all to themselves, so they decided to get rid of Willow. Gretel pushed Willow into the oven, and the naughty twins carried on wreaking havoc in her home. . .

. . . until it was bursting
with magic!

Willow's home collapsed.
It was only made out of
gingerbread after all.

And this time, Willow did get angry.

Because as it turns out,
Willow wasn't ALWAYS
a good witch.